TITCH

by PAT HUTCHINS

THE BODLEY HEAD
LONDON · SYDNEY · TORONTO

Copyright © Pat Hutchins 1971
ISBN 0 370 01137 6
Printed in Great Britain for
The Bodley Head Ltd
9 Bow Street, London WC2E 7AL
By William Clowes & Sons Ltd, Beccles
Published in New York by The Macmillan Company, 1971
First published in Great Britain 1972

For Darren

Titch was little.

His sister Mary
was a bit bigger.

And his brother Pete
was a lot bigger.

Pete had a great big bike.

Mary had a big bike.

And Titch had a little tricycle.

Pete had a kite
that flew high
above the trees.

Mary had a kite
that flew high
above the houses.

And Titch had a pinwheel
that he held in his hand.

Pete had a big drum.

Mary had a trumpet.

And Titch had
a little wooden whistle.

Pete had a big saw.

Mary had a big hammer.

And Titch held the nails.

Pete had a big spade.

Mary had a fat flowerpot.

But Titch had the tiny seed.

And Titch's seed grew

and grew

and grew.